Shoes Like
Miss Alice's

A Richard Jackson Book

Shoes Like Miss Alice's

by Angela Johnson

paintings by Ken Page

Orchard Books / New York

Orchard Books
95 Madison Avenue
New York, NY 10016

Manufactured in the United States of America
Printed by Barton Press, Inc.
Bound by Horowitz/Rae
Book design by Jean Krulis

10 9 8 7 6 5 4 3 2 1

The text of this book is set in 20 point Cochin.
The illustrations are oil paintings on canvas.

Library of Congress Cataloging-in-Publication Data
Johnson, Angela.
Shoes like Miss Alice's / by Angela Johnson ; paintings by Ken Page.
p.   cm.
Summary: A child spends the day with the lively new babysitter, Miss Alice.
ISBN 0-531-06814-5. — ISBN 0-531-08664-X (lib. bdg.)
[1. Babysitters — Fiction.] I. Page, Ken, ill. II. Title.
PZ7.J629Sh   1995
[E] — dc20   93-4872

To Dick Jackson—A.J.

To my pal, Allyson Page—K.P.

Miss Alice came on a cool day when the wind blew leaves up in the air.

Mama called to me, "Miss Alice is here to take care of you."

Mama put on her coat. She opened the door
and there was Miss Alice, the leaves,
and the wind all at once.

Then Mama was gone and there was no more leaves
or wind — just me and Miss Alice.

Maybe I could chase Mama . . .

. . . but Miss Alice took me to the window and waved
to her — so I did too.

Maybe I would go to my room and close the door
and think about when Mama would be home . . .

. . . but Miss Alice turned the radio on and started dancing.

"These are my dancing shoes, Sara," she said.

She twirled all over the room and danced
around the couch and caught my hand.
I danced a long time with Miss Alice.

We got hungry and ate a snack . . .

. . . but I got sad.

Miss Alice took her bag off the couch and pulled out some brown shoes and said, "Time to walk."

We walked in the wind and the leaves.

We walked past bridges and stores
and people.

I walked a long time with Miss Alice and then
we were home and tired.

When I pulled the covers over my head,
I missed Mama a lot and called for her.

Miss Alice sat next to me on the bed and said,
"I'll stay right here. I've got my nap shoes on."
They were blue and fuzzy.

I slept a long time beside Miss Alice.

When I woke up, Miss Alice and me drew pictures
of what we had done all day.

Miss Alice didn't have any shoes for drawing,
so she did it in her bare feet and so did I.

I drew pictures of Miss Alice dancing and sleeping.

Miss Alice drew pictures of me eating and laughing.

When Mama came, Miss Alice left in her walking shoes
with the wind and the leaves beside her.

I put my shoes on and danced through the house
making believe that they were shoes like Miss Alice's.